THAT DOCTOR
IN THE
ER

Rae T. Alexander

A Jo Danning
Short Story

1

Jo's Dream, Part One

2

Judy, Part One

3

Jo's Dream, Part Two

4

Judy, Part Two

5

Judy, Part Three

6

7

8

9

10

11

12

Judy's Finale

PREFACE

The subject of euthanasia shall remain a subject of controversy, even after reading this short story. This writing does not condemn or approve the practice. This is simply a work of fiction. However, it should be pointed out that there have been cases in the real world where profit and/or money have been the sole motivation to end a patient's life. In some cases, the wishes of the patient or family have been set aside for purposes of greed or convenience. May we all consider that, when dealing with suffering, we must include in the discussion the rights of the individual and the family. Human suffering is not pleasant, and assisted suicide may never be able to be viewed truly objectively.

While this story takes no position on assisted suicide, it does condemn forcing people into a decision because of a criminal or illegal motive, such as forced organ donations. No one should ever be forced to end their life.

-Rae T. Alexander

1
Jo's Dream, Part One

Fear…

I sat beside my bedroom mirror. I looked away in fear.

The terror within me grew in strength.

I was certainly not drunk. Wine had not touched my lips. Yet…my mind was like a lightning storm. My confusion was mixed with the pounding…pounding…pounding of my heart that seemed to increase in sound as the timeless seconds passed.

I was sincerely frightened, a rare trait for me. My military survival school once turned me into a tough girl, but that girl was not there. I looked at the ominous mirror in front of me. Its reflection brought me only pain. The image brought back memories that I buried years ago. I briefly looked at the figure a few moments before, but I promised myself—not again. The mirror showed a little girl that I very much detested. She was frail, and she never stood up for herself. That was the Jo that I hated, not the person that I became later, after years of defence training in the UK—well, that and living with a stubborn man without a clear ambition or a passionate drive—fighting had changed me. But *that* girl was nowhere to be found.

No one made me take that first glance. It was an accident. I was alone in my room except for my past fears that my agitated mind generated in an erratic world of a psychotic delusion.

My emotions were many, and I felt humiliated over my lack of control, especially after seeing such a cold reflection of part of myself that once lived inside a little girl that used to cry and miss her daddy while he was on his secret government "missions."

Memory is a funny thing when nothing is there but death and shame. Was *I* alive or dead, I thought. Could this be life anew?

I looked behind me, several steps away, and I saw two blurred and turned figures that suddenly appeared, showing me only the sides of their faces.

One was short, young, and trim. The other was tall and seemed handsome. My recollection left me, but, for a brief second, I thought I knew them once—the young boy and the man. They seemed to be looking at something. I was not quite sure if they were in front of a table or a bed, but that was what it seemed like—some elevated and draped rectangular object. They were bending down, looking at something, or, perhaps, someone.

They sobbed and sobbed and then cried more—the sound possessed an echo and muffle to it that made me feel as though I was inside a hollow box. I strained to hear their words, but a haunting silence took over…and then their images faded. I was soon alone again, except for my confused heart and personality.

After the two people disappeared, I was able to discern that I was in a white room with white walls and a brown door with a silver handle. Colors I could suddenly see—this was not possibly a dream, I thought.

The sound of my beating heart seemed to stop and a chilling silence filled the room. I gazed back at the mirror, as I sat on the cold floor. The antique frame of the mirror had an ornate framework around it. It was the type of mirror that I imagined belonged to a grandmother. It rested on a wooden stand that was darkly stained. I crawled toward the reflection and braced myself for the image, as I satisfied yet another urge to know the truth.

I tilted the mirror down, stared into it, and contemplated the horrific scene. The mirror did not display my likeness, or even the little girl; it showed an elderly man. His wrinkles sagged downward on his sad face. Where was the girl's image, I thought. I distinctly remembered that there was a girl in the mirror the last time I peered into the frightful shape. Was I mad?

The man held his side—as if he was in some kind of great pain. I could hear his intensive groans and low whimpers through gasps of shallow breath. Gradually, blood seeped through his fingers as he pressed into his body. He used both hands to stop the leaking and thick and oozing bodily fluid. He screamed in pain before reaching one of his hands toward me and through the mirror. He clenched his fist and then opened it up to form a shape.

It looked like a bear claw at first—but then it changed. He formed a different shape. That shape brought all of my memories back in an instant. I remembered everything, and I realized that I had to tell someone. I had solved a crime, but I was trapped. There was no one to tell. Memories of my entire life flooded my head, and I felt dizzy and elated at the same time. Knowing one's self is the highest joy and the greatest pain.

Suddenly, there was a knock on the door. I attempted to get up and walk, but I was unable to stand. I looked at my white and thin gown and naked legs and feet. The room became obscured by a white thick fog. I could scarcely make out the door, but I crawled toward it—dragging my numb legs. The knocking sound became a pounding sound. A voice behind the door cried out, "Mama!"

That voice brought a new and vibrant determination that increased my efforts and pace. It was Casey, my son.

2
Judy, Part One

First, she was my boss—in a way. Later, Jo and I became very good friends. There was, however, a bit of an age gap. I mean…I was a college teen, and she was a middle-aged lady. I was just her secretary, another co-op at the newspaper—until I walked into something that I should not have seen.

Jo Danning wrote an advice column and inspired me to change my major. I was always riveted by television criminal and lawyer programs before college, but Jo topped them all. She could solve crimes with a slight smell or a quick glance. The only problem with her abilities was that they were ignored and not nurtured, in my opinion. Although, I had no idea that crime solving was not her best ability.

The reason I knew about her criminal mind was because of our occasional banter that we had during our lunches together. On the days that she was in the office, she would insist on taking me for pizza or enchiladas. We would discuss the news of the day, and, many times, she would say the oddest things that turned out to be true—although it did not seem that way at the time.

I was not aware that she freelanced for a secret government agency that investigated the paranormal facts that surrounded certain crimes. We bonded during our favorite Italian and Mexican meals and discussed the latest crimes in the newspaper. I did not know that she was connected to several of the felonies that we often rambled on about. I found out that bit of information later.

Sometimes, we would have a guessing game. We tried to guess who the guilty party was, or what the outcome of the investigation was going to be. At future lunches, we would chat about our previous predictions. I was not always right, but Jo was usually accurate with her hunches.

One day, she lectured me about "reasoning."

"You rely too much on inductive reasoning, Judy," she said. "Generalization will often lead to incorrect conclusions. You should strive to use your deductive powers. In fact, you should have a creative blend of reasoning—but always trust deductive logic more than anything else."

At the cash register, soon after that discussion, Jo dropped her purse. Some matches fell to the floor, among other things. I helped Jo retrieve her spilled items and noticed the bold and glittering name on the matchbook cover. It read, "The Copa." It was the name of a new dance club.

The odd facts were that Jo did not smoke and the club was not even open yet. The Copa was supposed to open on Friday of that same week, according to the many advertisements on radio and television, and I felt compelled to question her about it.

"The Copa?" I asked. "What's up with that?"

"Oh, I'm doing a news story about the opening," she said, with some unusual and uncoordinated hesitation. "I'm going there Thursday night to finish an interview with the manager. I'm sure that's where I got these."

I should have left it alone. I should not have pursued the matter—but I was only following the prior instructions of my lunch partner. I was using deductive and inductive logic. And I had to know if I was correct or not. I suspected something was not quite right. I had to find out. Curiosity bit me with its annoying and infecting teeth.

I cut my Thursday night class in order to test my conjectures. I waited outside of the Copa, on the other side of a vacant lot. There were no lights on inside and no other cars parked around. Once I saw Jo's car pull up beside the club, I knew that I was right. She was not going to some interview. Besides, she was an advice columnist, not an investigator. My curiosity overwhelmed me. What was really going on, I wondered.

I should have driven away, but I got out of my car, with the intention of following her. I observed her from a safe distance. After a couple of minutes, I almost left before I saw the most curious action of Jo talking to herself, just outside the entrance to the closed club. She was having a conversation with someone, but I could not see anyone else with her. I thought, at least at that moment, that she was somewhat crazy. Maybe she has a variety of mental problems that I do not even know how to pronounce, I imagined.

I watched her say goodbye to the air. She waved to an invisible person, and then she got into her car and left. Upon seeing the gestures, I felt suddenly and extremely paranoid.

I first hid behind a brick wall, and then, later, a wooden box in the alley. I thought that I had avoided being seen. She could not possibly be waving at me; I knew that fact for certain. But I planned to question and interrogate her fully at our next lunch—although, I honestly had no clue on how to accomplish such a delicate task.

I imagined that I might say, "So, do you normally talk to yourself on dark nights, outside dance clubs? When did you take up smoking?" Why did she have matches in her purse? Jo hated the smell of cigarettes. And when she spoke about the matches there was an annoying jitter and delay, as if she was not telling the truth. I was dumbfounded, but I was addicted to the mystery. I needed to find out more, I thought.

I was suddenly startled by a tap on my shoulder, and I turned around, after an anxious shriek and an unconscious tremble.

The amazing thing was that I was brought into a new world from that moment on. I had just seen Jo get into her car and drive away—so what I saw next opened new eyes to the world of the mysterious and unexplainable. It went far beyond deductive logic.

The person that tapped me on the shoulder was none other than Jo Danning. A man ran up behind her with a drawn gun. I found out later that it was her friend, Ken, an agent for a paranormal branch of special government investigations that had no official name.

He looked at Jo and then at me and asked, "What the hell is *she* doing here?"

3
Jo's Dream, Part Two

"Casey, it's your mama," I said. "Open the door, honey."

I knew that he could not hear me. He did not respond. The door would not open either, despite obvious attempts from someone on the other side, turning the knob and twisting it with quick and forceful rotations. I heard the door and the metal handle shake inside of its frame—but the entry stayed closed. I was locked inside.

More objects began to appear, and some became much clearer than before. The fog slowly vanished, and it was obvious that I was in a hospital room. The bed became visible, and multiple monitors started to beep and flash.

But the inviting mirror was still in the corner, and I was drawn again to its magic—to the warning that it contained. I felt that the dispersing fog and the newly formed images represented the power of the dream fading—a chance to escape.

The bed was empty, but the sheets were folded down—like it was waiting for the next occupant, but the mirror still beckoned for my attention. I crawled to the oval shape because my legs were still paralyzed. I grabbed the sides of the stand and peered into the glass, but there was no longer a glass barrier, or even any type of a reflection within the wooden frame. It was a portal of some kind. I looked behind the stand and saw nothing but a hospital wall absent of windows. However, when I directly looked *through* the mirror, I perceived a dark hallway with a red light at the end of it.

I felt the back of the mirror with one hand. It was solid, and I could not see my hand behind it. I put my other hand inside the oval and reached into the hallway—the entrance to another world, it seemed.

Casey's voice and his knocking stopped, and I heard another voice beyond the closed door behind my back. I turned my head to the threatening sound.

"Jo Danning!" it said. "I have your son, and I will soon have you!" The gruff voice was male and familiar. I remembered hearing it just before I entered the dream. But was I alive? I wanted to find out. I had to take a chance. Did he truly have my son? Or was my protective mind projecting the fear? There was no time to debate the reality of the proclaimed kidnapping. A perceived danger was more than enough motivation, and I had to do something.

Since the door was not an option, I decided to try the only other exit out of the room with no windows. I reached into the oval with one arm and then another. I crawled over the bottom edge of the mirror and then pulled my legs into the hallway and away from the white room. As soon as I did, the mirror vanished, and I was in the dark corridor without a retreat.

My legs became warm, and they cramped, as spasms jerked my lower limbs in opposite directions for several seconds. I touched my legs and found that I could feel them again. I massaged them and felt the relief of gaining control—until I heard the haunting voice.

"Hello, Jo," the doctor said. He was at the end of the hallway, just under the red light. After my eyes adjusted to the darkness, I saw the surgical clothing. He wore a gown, cap, and mask and walked slowly toward me. He held up his right hand and displayed a syringe. Liquid shot upward as he primed his weapon.

"I think that I need to give you another shot," he said, as he took his other hand and scratched his mask and then his grayish hair that protruded under his surgical hat. "The gas is also having very little effect on you." He continued his trek away from the red light, moving steadily toward me.

I made an attempt to stand up, but I landed with the pain of another spasm.

"You need to take it easy, Jo," he said in an eerie and calming voice. His syringe trembled—a shake that resembled a Parkinson's tremor. He stepped up closer and knelt down in front of me.

"This will make you feel better. I promise," he said, as he outstretched his needle toward my sweaty neck.

I teased him, "Let me get my hair out of your way." I lifted my blonde hair and looked up with a flirt and a smile of surrender, but then I took my chance. I bolted up, knocked him down, and sprinted with an awkward limp in my left leg. I headed for the red light and a door just underneath.

I continued to limp, even after I was through the door. My legs burned as I pushed forward. I turned back once or twice to see if I was being followed, but there was no sign of the mysterious surgeon. I was in another corridor.

The hallway ended with another red light and a door that said, "ROOF ACCESS." The stairs were difficult to climb, but I was determined to work out the stiffness and gain full control of my legs. I exited the stairway, and I was nearly blinded by the light. It was daytime, and I was on a hospital roof.

I hurriedly hobbled on the uneven gravel and to the edge. I looked down and all around me. I was definitely in Wilmington, North Carolina. I could see the parking lot. I was so delighted at seeing something real that I started to cry and laugh uncontrollably. I yelled out my victory for the entire world to hear, although, there was no one around to listen to me—which was odd.

There were no people walking on the streets below. In fact, upon second glance, the cars did not quite seem real at all. The parking lot contained many duplicate red subcompacts and black boxlike cars. It was a nightmare that refused to end.

I was shocked out of my considerations, however, when I abruptly heard the chunky and painted gravel move behind me. It was the doctor. As I turned around, he quickly and gently pushed me over the edge. I fell backwards with my hands reaching upward. I was no match against gravity and no sense of balance. I saw him grin, as I started my plunge of death, on my way to the hot and the uncaring concrete walkway.

4
Judy, Part Two

After I witnessed the voodoo of the identical Jo and her matching car, I was escorted by Agent Ken Jackson to a holding cell. The incarceration took place in a small office with a table and four chairs, inside a downtown Wilmington office building. They were obviously not used to taking prisoners as both Jo and Ken offered me something to drink and initiated small talk about a local sports team and the weather. After their brief chat concluded, they excused themselves only for a few minutes to discuss what they referred to as their "dilemma." The heavier questions began after they returned.

"Judy, I had no idea that you would take me seriously enough to follow me tonight," Jo said.

"So, it was *your* fault, eh?"—Ken accused Jo, with a stare filled with judgmental condemnation.

"I don't understand why you have to even hold me," I added. "Ok, I saw something that I should not have. Who *are* you people?"

Jo ignored Ken's sign language that motioned and demanded caution.

"The simplified version is that I was hired by Ken and the government to consult in criminal investigations," Jo said. "I have certain … abilities … to see things."

"Like a psychic?" I asked. "Or, do you mean like turning into two people at once?" My mouth spilled sarcasm and veracity at the same time.

"What is she talking about?" Ken asked. That is when I knew that Jo and Ken did not always see the same things—or discuss the discrepancies. Jo must not be telling Ken the truth, I thought.

I found out, during my interrogation meeting, that Ken was at the club to observe and insure Jo's safety during a supposed interview with a member of a local hospital. However, Ken never saw the other Jo or the car in front of the club—but Jo had seen the same thing that I did. Ken was in the dark.

"You saw it too, didn't you?" she asked me. "I was hiding and saw someone that looked like me and someone that drove the same car." Jo looked at Ken who sat to her right.

"I did not see anyone from the hospital, Ken," she confessed to the agent. "I saw something else."

"What?" Ken asked. "You both saw something weird? At the same time?"

"Alright, Judy," Ken gave up and looked at me. "Since you seem to be a team member now—I need to do a background check and…"

"Shut up, Ken," Jo interrupted and then turned to me. "Judy, Ken was working on a case about the rise of questionable deaths and possible assisted suicides at Wilmington-Dixon General Hospital. I was assigned to interview a few doctors and see what I felt—if anything."

"So, you *are* a psychic," I said and smiled with a glance of victory, thinking only of my new logic and the endless possibilities of solving puzzling crimes.

"No, not really," Jo said.

"You remember the movie?" Ken interjected. "She sees dead people." Ken got up and asked us if we wanted pizza. He reached for his phone to place a delivery order, but Jo insisted that Ken should take care of the food personally—while she ironed things out with me. He left with somewhat hesitating and unbelieving eyes and a flirtatious wink, but, ultimately, the agent submitted to his blond and confident consultant. After Ken closed the door, Jo moved her chair away from the opposite side and sat beside me.

"Judy, I also saw her two nights ago—the same woman," she said, as she looked down on the floor and rested an elbow on the table and held her head as if in pain from a headache. "I have seen many things that I have never told anyone about. This case was not all that unusual—except for the fact that I saw myself...or, at least, someone that *looked* like me."

Jo told me that she first received a phone call from someone that *sounded* like her. The call was difficult to make out because there was construction noise in the background. The voice was screaming for help and yelling out the name of her son, Casey.

She also told me of a letter that she received in the mail that had the club's name on it, along with a scribbled message. The note was accompanied by a book of matches, from the Copa. And finally, she told me about a lady that wore a white gown and looked like her. She saw her running down a street close to the hospital—but she was too far away to make out the details of her face.

"Those matchbook covers have not been printed yet," Jo said. "I checked with a local print shop who told me that the order was delayed. The matchbooks will not be ready until next week."

"So..." I gulped. "You see dead people?"

"Yes, Judy," Jo confessed. "Sometimes I do."

"Why did *we* see something that Ken did not?" I asked her.

"Judy," Jo said and sighed. "People in life see what they wish, and nothing more—never forget that."

♦　♦　♦　♦

It was about a week later, after the late-night conversation and cheap pizza and soda, that I entered a school playground with the hopes of locating Jo's son. I found him at the gym, just after observing a few minutes of basketball. He wasn't playing; he was filling up water bottles. I wondered what gifts *he* possessed, and then I fumbled a short introduction. I briefly mentioned that I was his mom's secretary, and I had to explain what a co-op student worker was and how I assisted the staff at his mom's place of employment. My next sentence was rude and swift; however, I did not know of any other way to say it.

"Casey," I said, with my left hand on his shoulder. "Your mom's in a coma."

5
Judy, Part Three

"Do you like John?" Casey asked me. I rarely attempted to navigate the insane Wilmington traffic and answer questions that led to hypothetical questions at the same time, but I took the bait.

"Yeah…I guess he's ok," I told him. Truthfully, I was never fully acquainted with Mr. Graham. He was never "John" to me. He was just—Jo's boyfriend—a painter during the day, and a law school student at night. That was the only interesting but inconsequential detail that I knew.

John Graham only ate lunch with Jo on occasion. Mr. Fisher, Jo's boss, managed to give Jo extra projects that filled most of her day and her lunchtime with extracurricular deadlines. She also managed to write a few special-interest stories, in addition to a regular advice column. After all, Casey and life were expensive, and the alimony from her military man was often not quite enough. She quickly settled during a nasty divorce proceeding on a meager amount—her only concern was the sole custody of Casey. She did not want a drunk and a cheating husband to ever put his hands on her boy. When it came to Casey, Jo was extremely narrow-minded.

"Do *you* like him?" I asked, returning the question about John.

"He's ok, I guess," Casey said. "But I like Ken better—even though my mom is totally clueless about his feelings for her."

"Clueless?"—I was beginning to be reeled in. He was speaking my language. We seemed to agree with our assessment of Ken's character.

"Yeah," he began. "Ken likes her…rather a bit too much."

What bothered me more than anything was the idea that Casey was calm about a matter of life and death. He did not even inquire as to his mother's condition—except to ask, "When did it happen?"

I changed the subject abruptly, sensing his denial or possible aversion.

"Casey, what was life like in England?" I asked.

"You mean Suffolk?"—Casey's concentration level rose, along with a youthful and confused brow. "You aren't curious at all?"

"About?" I asked, as I turned into the hospital parking lot.

"You think that I don't care about my mother," he said. "When in fact, I actually love her very much."

My experience in the paranormal world was only in the world of fiction—up to the point of seeing Jo's double. I had the feeling that Casey was going to tell me that *he* had magic as well.

"Are you special?—like your mother?"—I had enough of hiding my inquisitive soul. Casey looked through the front window and stared at the concrete wall as I parked. He processed my last few questions for an answer.

"My dad was gone most of the time," he said. There were no tears as he continued. "He didn't love mama. He cheated on her. She never told me. I just knew it. I was glad to leave that place and come to North Carolina—even though I was scared at first."

He turned to me and finished his answer.

"I never told her," he said. "Whenever she was gone, I could sense that she was alright. She was on airplanes a lot, but I always knew that she was alright."

I was unable to determine if Casey was in denial of any kind of unresolved pain or if he just was not the type of kid to process danger properly. Casey was definitely not like other kids. In fact, *he* was more grown-up than *I* was. There was only about a distance of six years between our ages, but my nineteen seemed ancient. And yet, he seemed older at times. Silence has a way of making all of us wiser than we truly are.

"*You* are the one that is in denial," he blurted out.

Was my cover blown, I thought. Had he actually read my mind, I wondered.

"You *are* a witch, aren't you?" he insisted. "My mama sees things. I just have a connection to her. I am nothing special."

I was not convinced. He was not ordinary, in my opinion, and perhaps there were reasons for that.

Casey must have endured some abuse from his dad. I could sense it. The way that he shortened his sentences and thoughts to only the practical when confronted with a painful situation was the first clue. The second was his inability to have what I considered normal fun—for a boy his age. His hobby and love of botany was quite unusual. His dislike of sports and his reclusive preference for documentaries over partying with a bunch of friends were other things that bothered me. I never went to the extent of calling him "gay" like some of the children at his school did. I merely considered Casey different. It bothered my ordered and prejudiced mind.

"Look, Casey," I said, as I turned off the engine and lights. It was daylight, but the car garage was quite dark. Under other circumstances, witches and the dark would have gone together quite perfectly. "For the last time—I am *not* a witch."

"Then why is your nose bleeding?" he smirked and said.

An instinctive and reactive hand hit my face. I reached for my nostril and felt the liquid. I did, in fact, have a nosebleed. I quickly grabbed a tissue from my purse and wiped the blood off my fingers. I held the tissue at the end of my nose for a few seconds, while staring at Casey with my alarming eyes.

"I think that you should stay away from doors today," Casey said.

I felt as though the whole conversation had not even taken place. I could not put his words and attitude into a realm of reality that I could understand. Perhaps, I thought, I could only accept the fictional version of the strange.

I would have dismissed his remark entirely; however, the next event at the opening doors of the hospital prevented that from happening. We walked to the sliding glass doors. And, for a brief moment, for only half of a second, the doors jammed. I barely caught myself before I hurled my face into the glass. I looked down at Casey to find a reaction—perhaps an "I told you so."—but there was nothing. He was playing a video game on his cell phone. At least, that was what I thought he was doing. For all of his babble about witches, he could have been texting his mom, expecting a quick response from a comatose parent.

The doors finally opened, and we walked to the elevators. He was in *his* world, and I was not sure that *I* was in *any* world.

Just before the elevator opened on the third floor, and taking advantage of our brief privacy, I asked him a rather direct question.

"What is *your* power?"—I had not even meant to speak it. I was in deep thought, and it came out accidentally.

Casey stopped his game and tucked his phone into the front pocket of his jeans.

"I don't know that I have *any* powers. But I do know that faith and proof cannot live in the same house. So, who knows about anything—

sometimes…"

"Faith and proof?" I asked. "Who said that?"

"My mama," he said.

Once inside the hospital room, we found Ken waiting on us. He stood beside Jo's bed. His arms rested on the covers near her arm. His watery gaze and trembling lip under a greasy nose was the first thing that I noticed. His eyes were fixed on her limp hand, as if he wanted to hold it but could not. Jo's nose was the second item that I observed. Somehow, I was focusing on noses because of my earlier incident. I could not help but think of Casey's accusations, especially after I performed my next action.

I walked to the bed and reached my hand to Jo's face. I wiped a small drop of blood that exited her narrow nostril, and then I showed it to the agent.

I remembered my first interaction with Ken. My interrogation led to nothing but a late-night stomach ache from greasy food and carbonated beverages, and the persistent avoidance from the agent that did not want to tell me everything about his secretive organization. I remembered that Jo only told me as little as possible and discouraged me from asking any further questions after that night at their office, but I was newly determined to get in on the action and wanted to be part of the team.

"I think you should have this tested, Ken," I said to him.

6

Jo awoke and found herself in an operating room. She only *thought* that she had died. Her mind told her that it was all a dream, but what she saw convinced her otherwise. Two nurses in blue gowns prepared sterile instruments on tables to her left side. Above her face was a blinding light. She was draped in blue covers, and the whole room had various rectangular shapes with black, yellow, and white cords protruding from their edges. The doctor seemed to be bothered by noise and a faint knocking sound outside, or perhaps in the ceiling. Jo was not certain of the location of his concern because his eyes darted all around before speaking to her.

"Ah…you woke up," the masked doctor said to her, as he poked his head down, in-between her and the lamp. "You are going to be just fine—after a very short operation. We are—going to remove some things."

He paused briefly and said, "I think I heard someone outside."

"A little boy," he continued. "Is that your son? You *do* have a son, correct? I think I heard you mention it when you spoke to me. Or was it when he sent you a text message? But don't worry. Just, go to sleep. Go to sleep, Jo Danning."

The state of her usually sharp mind had been altered. She lay on a cold table. The confusion at that moment frustrated her. She knew that she had to get help. The surgeon in the room was the same one that chased her earlier. She needed to speak to Casey, or even Ken, but she had neither the strength nor the will to do so.

She drifted again into another drug-induced trance. Perhaps, she thought, the other world could help her, as her eyes closed softly. The scene quickly changed from one reality to another.

She forced open her stubborn eyelids, and then she jumped up from the pavement. She realized that she had just gotten up from her fall. She was back in her other previous dream. She looked up to the roof and saw the doctor staring down, and then she started her sprint toward her car. Her legs were completely healed. There were no longer any signs of paralysis. She darted to the parking lot to find her subcompact, but there were dozens of the same red car in the lot. Her task was more difficult than she imagined. This world must be an illusion, she concluded.

She knew that only *her* car possessed the item. It was a black stone, a tourmaline. The rock was on a plain black string, and it hung from her rearview mirror. She had to find the stone. The car with the stone would take her away from the doctor. The rock contained mystical powers. Somehow, she remembered that. Although, she could not remember where she first picked it up. Perhaps, it was from a candle store that bore the name "Wiccan." She could not remember. One thing was certain, it was the one item that singled out *her* car.

The odd fact was that Judy had once been complimented concerning the rock, as it hung on the teenager's neck at the newspaper office. Judy gave the stone to Jo, attempting to make friends. But for Jo, there were often reasons for everything, even when there were not. Jo believed in something called destiny, only because she experienced events that seemed to validate such ideas. But, at the same time, her logical mind argued against the thought of ghosts, superstitious objects, or various apparitions that had the ability to conduct a crime scene all by themselves. However, most of the time, Jo felt that everything happened for a reason—whether it was a phantom in the night or a gifted stone.

Her bare feet were pierced by random and discarded trash—bottle caps and broken glass. She tried every car on the first row. No string hung from the mirrors. The cars that she approached did not belong to her. No doors opened.

It was not as if she could start it, even she *could* find the correct one and open the door. She had no keys. She knew *that* particular fact was certain. Yet, she continued to try every door. It was not even logical. It was not like her to ignore the truth and the facts, but this was a world that was absent of them. She reminded herself of her own favorite line, "Faith and proof cannot exist together in the same room."

Or, can they? Maybe I should test that theory out!

As she stood in her gown with bleeding and blackened bare feet firmly planted, pondering the philosophical puzzle, she heard one of the cars start its engine. A flash of red was seen out of the corner of her eye. The speeding vehicle tore out of its space and headed straight for her. The sound of the engine increased as the driver pressed the pedal down all the way to the floor. The brakes screeched as the car spun around just in front of her— missing her by inches.

Jo stepped out of the car, but it was the other one. Both of them faced each other and dared the other to take the next step. The Jo from the car was dressed in a black leather jacket and black sunglasses. She wore military boots and a pistol on her side. The image seemed to shock the Jo that wore the white gown. Not only did the driver look like Jo, but she also wore her father's clothes, it was a psychological mockery of some kind. Was it her brain telling her to give up?

The sound of the padded feet of the surgeon interrupted the showdown. He panted for a moment as he stopped in front of them both. The sprint from the roof to the parking lot exhausted the old man.

"You did not have to run," the Jo near the car said. "She is quite harmless. Look!"—she pointed to the other Jo's face.

The barefooted Jo reached up to her nose and felt the blood, and then she held out a clawed right hand in front of the doctor.

"That will not work, my dear," the doctor said. "You cannot possibly…" He stopped his sentence as he saw the car and the other Jo vanish. Her dream power, whatever it was, was working. Jo was testing a theory.

"Perhaps…faith comes…just before the proof," Jo said, as she intensified her projection and the shape of her hand.

◆　◆　◆　◆

Casey finished his cry. He had feelings after all. Judy was pleasantly surprised—and relieved. Jo's son stood up beside the bed and looked at Ken.

"Mama is in danger, Ken," he said. "I feel it. She is trying to talk to us and tell us something."

Ken composed himself and found a chair near the window, avoiding Casey's emotional and illogical request. Besides, he thought, Jo was in a coma. She could not even save herself—let alone…solve a murder mystery. Casey marched out the door and left both Judy and Ken to fight it out.

"He's only a boy," Judy said. "Give him a little hope. He still thinks magic can cure the world."

"You know how he is, Judy," Ken said, as he stretched his feet out on top of the air conditioner vents near the window curtains. "He is weird sometimes—just like his mom."

"You're jealous!" Judy said and giggled.

Earlier, John Graham burst into the room and accused Ken of using Jo as bait to trap a killer. John had found out, through Casey, that Ken and Jo were investigating recent deaths at the hospital. Casey eavesdropped one night—and heard too much. John was told that Jo was moonlighting as a cop and it pissed him off. He fired off expletives in the hospital room at Ken before leaving in a rage. Afterward, Casey collapsed on his brain-dead mom and cried unlocked tears of release.

"I'm not jealous," he denied. Was John more caring about Jo than her boss was, he thought. "And I had nothing to do with this. It was just a car accident, according to the doctor who witnessed the accident outside of the emergency room. The police said that there was no foul play. The doctors here have all checked out. All I have are dead ends. This is usually the time that Jo helped me the most—when I had dead ends. Now, she is gone. The doctors have talked about waiting for a few weeks and then pulling the…" Ken was attempting to believe in the impossible, but that was usually Jo's job—not his.

Ken turned from Judy and saw Jo's hand. It was in the shape of a claw. For once, Ken imagined that he would be the hero in a case—with Jo's help, of course.

He got up, went quickly to the bed, and pointed out the clawed hand to Judy.

"Maybe it means that Jo is not quite gone…she *is* helping us…and I know who to see next," Ken said.

"Who," Judy asked.

"Dr. Clawley," Ken said. "Claw? Clawley? That's close enough!"

"Guess that is why *you* are the agent, and I ain't," Judy said and frowned.

"Aren't!" Ken corrected with a fatherly curl of his condescending brow.

7

Ken reviewed the facts, as he knew them. One month ago, Ken received letters that indicated a possible problem at a Wilmington hospital. Ken's boss called him and told him that he had received a few complaints as well. The agent was ordered to investigate the increased number of what was referred to as "suspicious deaths." Ken interviewed all of the doctors that were remotely involved in any deaths that had occurred on the premises. And one week ago, Jo Danning, his moderately stubborn and attractive consultant, said that she was following a lead connected to a nightclub. It promised a possible link to the hospital case.

Jo told Ken not to worry. She also omitted having knowledge of the matchbook. She was planning to meet the club owner, who also happened to be a doctor at the hospital. The doctor claimed that she had information about the deaths. He remembered the conversation well.

"I want to talk to Dr. Yakan," Jo said. "Not only was she a doctor on staff during several deaths at the hospital, but she owns a new night club. I got a call unexpectedly, after making some inquiries at Dixon Memorial, in addition to your own, of course. She wants to break the case wide open, but she wants to meet me alone."

Ken was doubtful because Dr. Yakan was a prominent member of the Wilmington Community Church. She had already been questioned. It seemed, to Ken, that Jo was chasing a dead horse.

Ken recalled following her to the club, against her objections, but he remembered that he had stayed at a cautious distance. He watched as Jo knocked on the club door and then walked behind the building—which led to an alley that circled around behind him. They had driven separately. He hid behind a crate and observed nothing else—except the sight of the arrival of Judy. While both Judy and Jo claimed to see another Jo talking to herself, he had only seen the first Jo walk around the building, past a few lightning bugs in the humid night air.

The next day, after a night of playful interrogation of the innocent college student, Judy, the police reported that a person, identified as Dr. Yakan, was pulled out of Greenfield Lake. The doctor, according to the reports, was on a "church" outing and fell into some dangerous water. She was killed by an alligator. The creature, ten feet of death, crushed her skull during a freak accident—an ill-advised swimming stunt of some kind—and there were many witnesses to that misfortune.

All of the doctors and nurses were questioned. All leads, as Ken had claimed, were dead. The reports of the numerous deaths at the hospital were officially ruled to be coincidences. However, a few days later, Jo was in a minor car accident, a hit and run, and she immediately fell into a coma. John Graham pieced enough of the facts together, along with Casey's overheard phone calls from his mom—enough information for John to accuse Ken of killing his girlfriend, Jo Danning, by "forcing her to be an agent."

Am I on another wild and stupid chase? Where is she when I need her?

Ken looked down at his list of doctors.

Dr. Samuel Pique, Dr.Arnold Crabbe, Dr. Herbert Clawley, Dr. Greir, Dr. Feinstien, Dr. Roberts, Dr. Shane, Dr. Agnone, Dr. Fregene, Dr. Gail Yakan

Each of the doctors were on duty during the time of the questionable deaths. The fact was, however, the deaths were not all questionable by themselves. They were merely reported as being questionable. The number of reported deaths was fifty on one particular day, but the causes were all explainable.

"Are you here *again?*" Dr. Clawley yelled. He could see his repeated visitor through his open office door, and he was tired of all of the accusations. "Ms. Philips, let him in!"

Ken passed the secretary and seated himself in Dr. Clawley's office, as the sweating and bearded doctor slammed his door and returned to his desk to face more perceived threats from the "law." The doctor scratched his beard before beginning.

"Damn it, Mr. Jackson," his tirade began. "I am sick of seeing you, sir. Don't you ever get tired of coming to see me? You know that I have nothing to say to you. I haven't done anything wrong, and neither has the hospital!"

"I have another lead," Ken started. "Someone told me the name 'Claw' was involved."

"*That's* your lead?" Dr. Clawley said and laughed. He reached for a box of cigars and offered one to Ken. When the agent refused, Dr. Clawley lit up his tobacco and puffed and continued his chuckles for another moment. Ken noticed a sign above the doctor's head, neatly framed on the wall, that read, "Thank You For Not Smoking."

"Do you know how many people die in a hospital every year, Mr. Jackson?" he asked. "Thousands…literally thousands. All your 'questionable' deaths were natural causes or verified accidents. They were iron-clad!" He pulled a drawer open, retrieved a file, and slammed it on his desk.

Dr. Clawley mumbled as he considered the facts and the figures once again for the stubborn agent.

"Let's see now," the doctor said, as he exhaled some smoke into Ken's face. "Septicemia, old age, cancer, car accidents, heart attacks, house fires... everything is explained. What do you want from me? The number of deaths is not unusual in any way. It happens all the time—some days more than others. People die!"

After another puff, Dr. Clawley insisted, "Where is it? Let me see that list again."

Dr. Clawley was Chief Physician at Wilmington-Dixon General Hospital. He was also the husband of a politician. He had no idea what agency Ken was from, but he assumed it was the FBI. The doctor was determined to seek vengeance and Ken's job if the harassment continued.

"Dr. Yakan...deceased," the doctor started. He looked at the other names on the paper from Ken. The agent had reluctantly dug it out of his back pocket once again for the doctor to review. Ken recalled that he must have been in the same office at least ten times. They both were tired of the game. "Shane and Agnone—deacons in their church...Hell, Sam has been here for over twenty years, shaky when giving a shot, but an experienced manager. Greir, Feinstein...all men and women of excellent character with no criminal record. And if we were poisoning people we would be falling over from the rat poisoning. But we are mostly healthy, except for some dermatitis or rheumatism. You have nothing!" He slammed the file closed and yelled back, "Get out of my office!"

"All I am asking for is some help," Ken said meekly. His tough spirit was shattered by the loss of his partner. He was not his usual boisterous and obnoxious self. Had Jo been wrong, he thought. Maybe her hand gesture had been nothing more than a muscular reflex. Ken was losing hope...and faith.

"Maybe you need to see a shrink," Clawley said. "Go bother Dr. Crabbe. He has trained in the field of the mind… maybe *he* can help you."

Ken took back the paper that was thrown at him. He tucked his list back into his pocket and slowly stood, turned around, and left the doctor's office. His pocket vibrated and buzzed, and he reluctantly pulled out his cell phone. He found a bench in the lobby and read Judy's message in bold:

JO'S MIDDLE FINGER AND INDEX FINGER EXTENDED
DON'T THINK IT IS CLAW BUT THINK IT IS CRAB
CASEY IN TROUBLE!! MEET ME IN CAFETERIA!!!

8

"Are you going to pay for the damage, sir?" the head janitor asked Ken. The small café section of the cafeteria was splattered with enchilada sauce and other flavors. Workers were mopping up the disaster. "I may have to call the directors or the police…"

"No, don't," Ken hurriedly interjected. "I am sure we can work something out." He flashed a badge of authority, with little more than the word "Agent" on it, and told him that he would handle it personally, and then he handed him a hundred-dollar bill. It seemed to silence the director as he went back to the cleanup with no further complaints.

Ken motioned a quarantined Judy and Casey, who were both sitting in a corner, and they all left for the least likely place to be disturbed…the chapel. They found a seat near the back and talked amidst the sound of *Amazing Grace*. Casey sat between the teenager and the agent, as he began with more of an apology than an explanation.

"I couldn't help myself," Casey said. "I think that I just got so upset that I started throwing food all over the place. I don't want to lose my mama!" He leaned against Judy who took the next line.

"Can't you see what is going on?" Judy pleaded with Ken. "She is speaking through us… or *something* is. The claw? Remember? And now, it is Casey that she speaks to."

"Judy, calm down," Ken said and stood up. He gazed at the crucifix at the front of the room and shook his head. "What is she supposed to be saying? This is just another incident like the Copa, when you and Jo thought you saw something weird. Remember? I think that you have seen way too many movies, Judy. And I believe that I have seen too many weird things too. We all are so worried about losing Jo that we are jumping to conclusions, grasping for straws—and every other cliché that you can think of. *You* are not an *agent*, and, perhaps, I have seen so many paranormal occurrences that I am becoming unrealistically hopeful. There is no message. Jo is brain-dead!" He stopped, and then he realized the blunt words that were said in front of Casey. He started to apologize, but the faith of Casey prevailed.

"She is *not* dead!" Casey insisted. "My mama is alive…somewhere…and I am going to get her and bring her back—with or without anyone else!"

"Oh, my God!" Ken said, and he immediately darted a glance at the cross again.

"What about the claw thing? Did you speak to the doctor?" Judy asked.

"Dead end," Ken sighed and sat down. That word seemed to be the word of the hour—dead. He reached out to Casey, hugged him, and held him tightly. "I am sorry, Casey" he said apologetically. "I have tried real hard." Casey pulled away and wiped away his fresh tears.

"Did you talk to Dr. Crabbe? Judy said that she sent you a text," he said to an open-mouthed Ken.

"Look," Ken said. "You two are not agents and are not qualified…"

"Judy was right about you!" Casey said and stood up. He moved into the aisle and walked to the door. He yelled back, as he left the generic room of contemplation, "You *are* a moron!" Ken immediately looked at Judy, who lowered her head in embarrassment.

"In my defense," Judy said, as she lifted her blushing face. "I was being the 'good cop'… you know… the buddy?"

The agent's phone vibrated in his pocket as the incoming text broke up the premature celebration.

"DIAZEPAM," it said. It was from Annette, his assistance, back at the lab. Jo's blood tests were finished.

"Well, Judy," he said to her, jumping again to his usual and premature conclusions. "Looks like science is speaking to us, if no one else is… Jo was poisoned! And I bet there wasn't even a car, at least not one that touched her."

Judy's phone buzzed also, and she had news to tell as well.

"Well, we had a thief in the church!" Judy pronounced.

"What?" Ken asked as he took Judy's offered phone with the explanation.

The text read, "SORRY I TOOK YOUR WALLET. I AM GOING TO THE CLUB TO FIND MAMA!! DON'T TELL KEN!!"

"Crazy kid! His mom is in a hospital bed and he is running away from the trauma. You go find Casey, and I am going to see Dr. Crabbe," Ken said with disgust. Too many things were happening.

Where the hell are you, Jo?

Judy asked one last question from Ken before they left the chapel. She wanted to know what Doctor Crabbe's specialty was.

"He is in charge of organ donations to the hospital," Ken said.

9

Jo's car bumped the curve as she pulled into the space, just outside the Copa. The determination was there, but the memory of how she got there was absent. She surrendered to the idea of being inside a fragment of a dream—no beginning, middle, or ending.

She left her car and waited on the sidewalk, as a slight breeze blew an oversized shirt that she had stolen from a backyard. The words on the shirt said, "I really don't care." And it fit her mood. She was still barefoot, and the hospital gown was underneath her shirt and tucked into a pair of jeans. She wasn't sure where they came from, and neither did she remember putting them on. If this was a dream, she thought, the details were amazing.

She observed a narrow path around the club. It was a divided lane that led to an alley on one side, and to a wooded back lot on the other. The pavement was partially finished and the mailbox near the door of the Copa was stuffed with letters, a small parcel, and a stack of stamped envelopes left by the postal carrier. She noticed the date on some of the protruding letters to be a few weeks earlier than she thought it should be.

"Well, dreams can happen during any time and place, I suppose," she mumbled to herself. "Either that, or someone does not check their mail on time."

During a moment of curiosity, Jo tugged and bent the parcel to see who it was from. Unintentionally, she ripped and tore the small flat envelope, as she pulled it away from the sharp top edges of the mailbox. A book of matches fell out, and she caught them before they hit the ground. A print shop had sent the club a sample. As she looked at the name on the cover of the matches and then back at the stamped envelopes, she formulated a most ingenious way to send a message to someone outside of her dream world—and, at the same time, to test the theory about faith and proof.

"Maybe it takes faith to see the proof, or perhaps, proof to see the faith," she said to herself.

Fortunately, there was also a pen inside the envelope, another teaser from the print shop. She took the pen and the stack of envelopes from the mailbox. She wrote a note on one of the envelopes, stating that she was a member of the hospital staff with information concerning the deaths at Dixon.

She wrote, "Meet me here tomorrow night. Here are some matches to prove my connection to..."

She felt the presence of someone else. It was like that eerie feeling that someone was watching when there was no proof of that happening. She finished her note and then placed the note written on one envelope inside another stamped envelope. She started to rush across the street to mail the letter, but she saw a mailbox vanish. A construction sign took its place. There was a telephone booth that was there when she had first arrived—but it too vanished. The thought of calling for someone crossed her mind. Maybe I could find another phone down the street, she pondered.

She turned to the mailbox on the side of the club. It too had disappeared. In its place were the nails that used to hold it up. It seemed to have been ripped from the side of the house. Ken would have immediately assumed "cover-up." Jo, however, deduced that, once again, she must be slipping into another realm.

Perhaps, this was indeed a dream without mercy or escape, she thought. It was as if she had skipped to another time, for a brief moment.

However, she still held, in her trembling hands, the envelopes, pen, and matchbook. Her car was still parked next to the curb.

"Mama?" a voice beside her said. She looked to her right and saw Casey standing confidently on the sidewalk—alive, but out of breath. "I ran as fast as I could to get here. I *knew* you were here!" Jo could not decide if his appearance was an illusion or a miracle. She wondered if he had traveled a great distance—and how. Even Casey was puzzled.

If Judy wasn't a witch, then perhaps *he* had special powers of some kind, he thought. Casey remembered running, but not for miles and miles. But he tossed aside the idea of special powers when he decided that it was just the steadfast love of his mama that had performed all of the magic that was needed to reach out to him. Casey sensed his mama and her presence and location. However, he was not entirely inside of her world—he failed to recognize her parked car...that was because he could not even see it.

She knelt down and squeezed him tightly against her before standing up again and giving him a stern warning.

"You need to get out of here as soon as possible," she said. "It isn't safe, and I don't understand all of the rules here."

"I don't even remember how I got here," Casey said. "I was going to take a bus, just after I left the chapel. I turned into a corridor at the hospital and burst through a door. And what do you mean rules?" he said, slightly offended.

"I am in some kind of dream, or perhaps it is only *like* a dream, but with a partial reality to it," she added, choosing to ignore the hospital and chapel remarks. There were more than enough *other* mysteries going on at the moment.

As she spoke, the modulation of her words varied and became

extremely inconsistent. Distance formed and grew between the two worlds.

Casey's tightened expression showed confusion, as Jo's incoherent words attempted to explain everything that happened during her chase by the masked doctor. As she waved her arms and was about to speak the name of her villain, Casey vanished and his screaming of her name faded like a vapor.

"MAMA!"

He was gone, but a memory was triggered within Jo. She realized that *she* was the one that had waved her arms when Judy and her other self had seen the perplexing sight in front of the Copa. Jo somehow envisioned her way through time to give a clue that would be needed later. During some of her past encounters with spirits and ghosts, dead people had interacted with her to warn her or point her in the right direction—down the road that eventually solved a mystery. Now, it was Jo that did the same thing.

"Does this mean that I am dead?" she asked herself.

She did not have time to figure it out. She got into the car, drove away with the letter and other stamped envelopes, and found a post office about three blocks away. She mailed the letter that contained a warning and an invitation—and the matchbook. She also managed to write several other letters onto discarded papers thrown into a trash can. She used the stamped envelopes and mailed all of her messages of doom. She even found a phone, behind an unlocked office door, and she attempted to make a phone call for help. However, the phone did not seem to work—no one answered back, and static was on the line. The office showed evidence of being remodeled, and then it didn't. Paint brushes and buckets appeared and disappeared. Time seemed to go back and forth in this world. She felt as though her concentration was fading.

When she finally came out of the post office, she collapsed on the sidewalk from an intense pain inside of her head. She fell to her knees and awoke in a different world.

The masked doctor asked her, as she opened her eyes, "Are you in pain, my dear?" The doctor continued as Jo attempted to free herself from the restraints. "You were screaming, and we cannot have that, you know. You have an amazing tolerance to the anesthesia—an abnormal one, I think."

The pain increased inside of Jo. Her constant physical struggle on the table and mental objections within her mind were much too hard to handle for any great length of time. She relaxed and surrendered to the sleep, and she returned to her drug-induced coma. She hoped that the other Jo had heard her screams during her frantic and brief phone call—to herself.

Soon the doctor would begin to dissect her brain-dead body. Soon her organs would be on ice and on sale to the highest bidder.

10

"Dr. Crabbe," Ken said. "I just saw you cut into a human body, from the surgical observation deck. How do you do that and then eat?"

The doctor agreed to meet the disturbed and persistent Ken in the cafeteria, but only after a liver could be removed from a donor that had been pronounced dead in the emergency room. The man had signed a donor card several weeks earlier. Someone's life would be saved—and very soon. That was what it was all about—saving lives.

"How many times must you interview me?" the doctor said, as he smacked through his macaroni and cheese. The earlier antics of Casey, and whatever possessed him, had caused the café manager to remove enchiladas from the menu. Carbs, soda, and fried foods were the only items left.

"Clawley called you?" Ken asked.

"Of course, he did," Crabbe said with a full mouth. He swallowed and then gave Ken his own version of a Clawley rejection. "Mr. Jackson, mysterious deaths or the number of deaths just don't automatically add up to mischief or murder. You need to start chasing some real criminals. We *save* people here—we *save lives*. We don't *kill* people. And yes, Jo Danning having diazepam is totally normal—she was having seizures, according to her doctor. And I know you already talked to him, or at least to his nurses."

As the doctor stuck his fork into the bowl of cheesy noodles, Ken's mind went back to how he became sick during his observation. He watched the doctor make an incision and open a chest. An electric saw was used. And as the doctor cut the sternum, Ken saw layers of yellow fat, underneath the top skin. The tissue bounced as the surgeon's hands moved the intestines out of the way. The heart was still beating—it seemed to go down, and then it moved to the patient's right. It was a nauseating rhythm to the agent.

"When I operate, I do not see a human being," Doctor Crabbe said. "I care, of course. But when someone's brain is dead—that is different. I see the falciform ligament of the liver. I see bile ducts and other body parts—nothing more."

As the doctor swallowed his last bite, he leaned over the table, displayed bits of yellow pasta in the gaps of his teeth, and whispered, "You never told us the details of your concerns. What makes you believe that the hospital is killing all these people?" Ken turned his face away from the doctor's face while attempting a partial answer.

The agent explained that the most annoying challenge was the vagueness of the complaint and inquiry. The death count had been considered too high, at least, according to the complaints. Ken had to admit that all that he had was a stack of scribbled accusations, sent from anonymous sources, but he kept that fact to himself.

"I am sure that you interviewed the people who brought up the complaints?" the doctor asked.

"I can't tell you about the numbers or breach any privacy here," Ken said, as he turned and faced the doctor. "But I have my suspicions that it surrounds euthanasia—isn't that how you take a life, doctor?—like a dog or cat?"

The truth was that Ken, along with several of his superiors, received several anonymous tips from a number of people. However, the warnings were all in the same scrawled handwriting—barely legible, although, they could very well have been from either one person or several. They were different letters that stated that a brother or sister had died prematurely—or a mother or father had contracted cancer and wished for death. Somehow, someone was granting their wishes. The number of complaints was less than a dozen, but the method of the handwriting being very similar was something that presented a red flag that had to be checked out. However, Ken was almost satisfied, after hours of interviewing all of the suspects, that the letters were all written by a crackpot, someone wanting to stir up some trouble.

"I suppose that the only thing I really have are accusations—well, that and Dr. Yakan's dead body," Ken said.

The puzzled doctor thought for a moment and then said, "Dr. Yakan had bills, and she borrowed a lot of money from a lot of shady characters. She just wanted to start a nightclub, and medical bills stood in her way. But I guess you already figured that one out."

Ken knew that statement was true. Her death was ruled an accident, even though she had several notes in her apartment that seemed to tie her to a local crime boss who had money. For Ken, it seemed too easy, a diversion of some kind, but too many witnesses viewed her "accident." After the animal was shot and her body recovered from the water, the autopsy did not reveal anything in her system, except for the drugs from the tranquilizer guns that had contaminated her blood from the bites, along with the red water near the aquatic reptile that seeped into her wounds. If the "mob" or someone had killed her, they were experts at drugs. And that fact alone made Ken even more suspicious of doctors.

A despondent Ken looked down with disappointment. He once thought that Jo was trying to communicate with her hands—trying to send a message out. Judy had believed that, at least—even more than he did. A retracted finger, a clenched fist, and a vivid imagination spawned the fruit of the desperate, he thought. Ken was beginning to give up.

Ken stayed at the table while the doctor left. His glazed eyes and moodiness were not shaken as the doctor said goodbye and made a few remarks about getting back to the agent, if anything came up. Ken pulled out the list and crossed out all of the doctors' names.

Dr. Samuel Pique, Dr.Arnold Crabbe, Dr. Herbert Clawley, Dr. Greir, Dr. Feinstien, Dr. Roberts, Dr. Shane, Dr. Agnone, Dr. Fregene, Dr. Gail Yakan

It was over. Time for me to go see how Jo is doing, he thought.

◆ ◆ ◆ ◆

On the other side of town, after driving all around the hospital area and checking Jo's house, Judy managed to catch up with Casey, just outside of the Copa. The club's name was mentioned just enough in front of the boy to create a slight case of curiosity. And he was also a most stubborn son at times.

She parked her car, after navigating around some new construction cones. The entire street and a few others nearby the newly remodeled post office were being repaved soon.

She found Casey sitting on a curb. She conjectured that Casey, out of remorse, might have hitchhiked to the Copa. With money from her wallet, she thought, he might have even arrived by bus. Those methods of travel were more logical than the thought of him magically appearing there, mystically drawing Judy to the Copa to retrieve her wallet. She never asked, or perhaps she forgot to inquire. She decided to ignore the necromantic hypothesis once she turned off her engine and opened her car door.

She got out and walked toward him, immediately sensing that he was in another world. His silence and cold stare placed a barrier in front of her questions, but she tried anyway. But instead of an expected argument, Casey moved his hands together and then moved them outward to his side as he stood up.

"I had to come here," he said, as he handed Judy's wallet back to her. "I'm sorry. I was going to run away, but my mama told me to come here. Or, rather, I knew that she would be here…I don't know."

A scared Casey, worried about his mother, grabbed and hugged his new friend Judy, as she led him back to her car without an expected scolding or lecture. She decided to take Casey back to his house. The best thing was to distance themselves from the mysterious club, she thought. Neither of them observed the hiding eyes that were looking at them during their conversation. All of their words and actions were monitored by someone that chose not to reveal themselves.

Once she drove away from the curb of the Copa, Judy asked a question about the hand gestures.

"What was that you did?" she asked. "Back there, just a moment ago…what was that?"

"Sign language," Casey said. "It's from an extra-curricular course. Why?"

"I used to take sign language as a class myself," she said. "I dated this guy who…"

All at once, Judy's mind started to explode with endorphins. Jo's reminder to her about the importance of deductive logic had paid off. She figured the case out. For once, she thought, I know what is going on. She spun the car around, in the direction of the hospital.

Under her directions, she passed her cell phone to Casey and told him to text Ken.

The text read, "It wasn't a crab or a claw it was the sign for…"

Unfortunately, the cell phone battery died, and the text was never sent, and a sudden explosion from the front of the car made Judy pull over to the curb. She only managed to drive a few blocks away from the Copa before the blown tire forced her actions. Another vehicle, one that had been following her since leaving the club, immediately stopped behind her. A tall man exited and ran up to her side of the car.

Judy screamed in surprise when she saw the man—until she realized who it was. She rolled down her window and said, "You scared the crap out of me!"

As John Graham smiled at her, she added, "Were you *following* me? You *do* love her, don't you?"

11

Jo's left side was numb. She also continued fighting off the desire to sleep as she fell into one last dream. Her writing had been with the wrong hand because the other one had no feeling in it at all. It was the reason that her handwriting was not noticed by Ken. The content on the scribbled and barely readable letters that were mailed, each with her own accusations, had all been based upon what she heard the surgeon brag about.

He talked about declaring several people dead, in order to operate on them and remove some of their organs. The surgeon encouraged organ donations and played on people's fears—enticing each victim to end their life of pain, providing each one of them with an expedient and convenient method of performing their final deed on Earth. A few patients had cancer. Others had been DOA, the result of several random and unfortunate accidents. However, most of them were convinced that death was the only option for them. They were forced to die, and many of them needlessly and impetuously shattered the bonds of family members.

The doctor was once a veterinarian before medical school, an expert also with tranquilizers. He was even a member of Dr. Yakan's church, a convenient circumstance that allowed him to formulate and plan a well-organized and accidental death—with plenty of "Christian" witnesses.

Somehow, Jo performed actions that only her ghosts had done on her previous cases—she crossed the time and space barrier, physically altered paper, with a magic pen and ink, and sent messages from the dream world to the real world. Although, she often wondered what the difference was between the two. How can anyone prove that one place or time is more reliable than another, she thought. Reality has always been tied to perception—at least, she found this to be true. And faith and proof were more attached than anyone could imagine. In the end, she was more confused than she was sure of anything. Dreams tend to do that; they tear up the soul, spirit, and mind, and then they spit or vomit up the results for the worried being to decipher. Ultimately, we must all choose our own reality. We must individually determine the worth of our own frame of reference.

Jo's letters included no fingerprints, and her clues that she planted under great internal pain and stress were chaotic at best.

One of her letters read:

DOCTOR BAD, VESTIGATE ANGER CHILE
DOCTORS KILLING PEOPLE
HELP

There were several letters similar to this, all in the same left-handed writing that Jo etched out on the paper from the Copa mailbox and mailed in the pre-stamped envelopes. That is what started the investigation…simple letters sent to Ken's secret organization by one of his operatives…Jo Danning.

As Ken reviewed some of the letters in his mind one last time, he kept asking himself a question. He left the cafeteria and repeated, "What would Jo do?" He even asked himself, "What would Casey do?" He was not oblivious to the fact that both Jo and her son possessed incredible gifts. Even though Casey was not an agent, he had been most helpful with his knowledge of botany. Jo's knowledge of language and Casey's love and adoration for plants and all things "green" frequently combined to break a case.

"What would Jo do? What would…" His mumbling in the parking lot was so loud, that an orderly asked him, just before Ken got into his car, "Sir? Is everything ok?"

"Just a little peaked," Ken said. "It's been a long…" Ken stopped and excused himself before blasting out of the parking lot ahead of burning tire rubber. He figured it out—finally!

He quickly called John Graham and pleaded with him to find Judy and Casey. The plan was for John to check Jo and Judy's house and for Ken to check the Copa.

"John, I will explain later," Ken yelled into his plastic cell phone. "Find them both, if you can. I will meet you at the Copa."

John had called in sick for the last two days. His paint jobs would have to wait. Finding out that his girlfriend was in a coma, after seeing her healthy the week before, was too much for him. John did not meet many women at his age. Jo was a gift from heaven that was taken away from him much too soon. He later found and tailed Judy's car and eventually parked his car beside a curb that Judy pulled next to as a result of a flat tire.

Ken's phone buzzed after his call to John. It was Dr. Crabbe. His news widened the mystery.

"Mr. Jackson," Dr. Crabbe said. "Jo's gone from the hospital. She checked out, it seems. I thought you should know." The doctor had a new tone—one that seemed helpful and apologetic.

"Thank you, Dr. Crabbe," Ken said, as he prepared to end the call abruptly. "I know where she is!"

Ken remembered Casey bugging him for help on a spelling bee, during a night that he played the role of "babysitter" for Jo, in order for her to enjoy the company of John.

Ken's car spun around the narrow street corners, as he fully accelerated his antique sports car. His destination was 1356 Ireland Street. However, the name was partially covered from the recent splattering of tar and dirt by construction crews. It read, "Ire Street."

The new construction on that street, pursued feverishly by a local bureaucrat, had seriously delayed an intended opening day. The business seemed to be nothing but a vacant property. However, inside the sleeping establishment, there were unscrupulous practitioners of a different type of demolition—the destruction of innocent and sacred human flesh. A mailbox was torn off the front of the building, just beside of the front door, exposing nails and sharp and jagged wood. The residents inside secured a private postal box nearby because, apparently, some of their mail had been recently stolen.

"I hope I am not too late," Ken said, on his way to the Copa.

12
Judy's Finale

I never saw a "bust" before—not in real life. The action and drama on a television screen did not compare to the lack of excitement of "being there." I found that the experience was much faster than a dramatized version. I was expecting to see Ken or John break down the door and yell out something like, "Open the door, you son of a bitch!" I was expecting to see guns blasting and hear villains cussing.

Instead, Ken and John, after arriving at the Copa, and knocking and yelling for a few seconds, simply entered quietly, just after the lock was picked. Once inside, they found that Doctor Pique had committed suicide. It was not until his body was covered and Jo was found and taken out of the basement that I was privy to further information.

Jo was taken back to the hospital in an ambulance. Later, Ken asked the administrator for a more private hospital room. The hospital, fearful of a lawsuit, placed her in a room that was usually reserved for VIPs and Government officials. Ken, John, and Casey stood around Jo's bed, as I took notes nearby and interjected some occasional insights of my own.

Dr. Pique was a silent partner with the Copa. He also had a gambling addiction and an expensive lifestyle that he financed by arranging organs to be sold in exchange for his soul. The barter became so lucrative that he was unable to find a stopping point. His partner, Dr. Yakan, had unpaid lawyer bills, from a tedious and drawn-out divorce, and massive educational loans. The gambling debt evidence that was planted in her apartment only served the purpose of diverting Ken away from Dr. Pique. Additionally, it was concluded that Dr. Yakan was shot and killed by a silent and single bullet, fired out of a rifle with a silencer from a hidden position. The wound was destroyed after the jaws of the alligator tore away the flesh. The rifle with the doctor's prints was found in the basement, and a casing was found near the woods, not too far from the lake. Dr. Pique loaded his weapon with tranquilizer bullets, just before he hid behind a tree during a church outing that he had officially never attended. His nurses provided assurances of that fact. "He was in the emergency room at that time," they claimed. The diazepam in the bullet caused Dr. Yakan to stumble, an action that everyone else thought was an intentional dance or dare, near a pool of shallow water. The alligator was conveniently released, by another assistant that was part of the conspiracy, from a nearby zoo observation area. It had all been carefully arranged by Dr. Pique.

Dr. Yakan's conscious needed to be dealt with—and, in the most final and severe manner...murder! She was going to report Dr. Pique to the authorities, hoping for a plea bargain. That was Ken's guess, at least. The club was to be both a front for money laundering as well as the top floor of a building that housed illegal and unauthorized euthanasia in the basement. Although many signatures for donations were forged, many times the doctors became convinced that their deeds were in the best interest of the community and served a greater need—to end the needless suffering of the dying or the inflicted. Finally, however, it was Dr. Pique's inability to face his own actions that led to his suicide—forcing many of his patients to take unnecessary journeys to the unknown regions of the dead.

The doctor left a suicide note that filled in many of the details. The note was a scribbled one, but readable, a confession to go along with a corpse. The police that investigated the scene concluded that he went mad with guilt, but I preferred to imagine strange powers beyond the grave, or his control, forcing him into writing the note—threatening him with more hell if he did not obey the spirits. Perhaps the criminal heard the tears of a child and the desperate cries of a mother—two of the most powerful forces in the universe.

"Dr. Pique had a self-inflicted bullet wound to his head, and his nurses were found and arrested," Ken said to us. "The doctor recruited people that needed money..." Ken wanted to add that some of the nurses were merely the doctor's former veterinary assistants with forged licenses and names, but that would have made him and his department look grossly negligent—so he omitted the information. That part came out much later during the many hearings concerning the "Great Hospital Scandal of Wilmington," as the locals called it. Fortunately, it was determined that the local police had botched the investigation, and not Ken's team.

Jo was awake and out of her induced coma. She was no longer under the care of Dr. Pique, the emergency room doctor that first admitted her. During an earlier interview with Jo, behind a pulled screen curtain, the doctor drugged her with a sudden and surprising prick of a needle and loaded syringe. Her cell phone was open as the doctor placed her on an exam table. Her phone displayed a text message from Casey stating, "I hate spelling, Mom!"

"Yes, well it took you all long enough!" Jo said, as she raised and adjusted the height of the bed. She wanted to see everyone's faces as she regained her full awareness.

John Graham, her middle-aged laborer and sweetheart, squeezed her hand and rubbed her shoulder. His gray hair blended into his worry lines under his eyes and on his brow.

Casey stood at the end of the bed, until Jo called for him to come closer.

"My hero!" Jo said to him as they embraced. The action seemed to make Ken envious, and I thought I saw a hurtful tear. Ken later boasted to me about his ability to crack the case and figure it all out, but I believed that in his heart he was not the arrogant guy that he sometimes pretended to be.

It seemed that the pieces of the puzzle were scattered about. The claw, the sign language that came from Jo's hand, represented anger or irritation. The street name matched that as well. However, the enchilada incident was less clear. Jo believed that her dream thoughts caused Casey to toss the food in relation to what she was thinking of at the time—Chili pique plants—the closest thing to the concept of irritation and the doctor's name that she could imagine—hot and spicy. In addition, Casey recently made a spelling mistake on what he considered to be a very simple word—irritation. She had hoped that Ken and Casey would talk and figure it out. She always thought that those two could help each other with their own individual and delicate states of emotional immaturity. Casey had an excuse; he was still a child. But Ken was just a sheltered little boy with very little social skills when it came to people. She often wondered how he even got his job. She later told me that it would be an interesting story for him to tell her one day—or another time. But what was time and logic to a woman who was barely able to look inside the enigma of a time and death barrier, I wondered. Of course, it was a long time before Ken finally admitted that he first stumbled onto the solution by being "peaked," a word that merely rhymed with the doctor's name. As for Casey, it was all about the pique plants that he was studying that week, and his failure to tell Ken about the connection. Ken hated botany; he thought it was a boring subject for a boy to waste his time with. I believe that it bothered Casey for some time—not telling Ken about his thoughts earlier on. As for me, I suppose that my bloody nose forced the attention to Jo's dripping nasal fluid that also provided another clue. Jo's attempt in providing an orderly message or neatly stacked set of clues had failed, but the objective was accomplished all the same.

To score further points with Jo, and everyone else in the room, Ken exaggerated his knowledge of something called a "claustrum" and how it controlled consciousness. He was back to his old self.

Jo shut Ken down rather quickly and said, "Been on the internet, eh?"

Ken blushed and excused himself for an important call when he saw John and Jo perform an extended and loud kiss. Casey and Ken and I went into the hallway and provided Jo with more privacy. Ken pulled me aside, just outside of her door, and gave me a flirting smile and a wink.

"You know, this *still* doesn't make you an agent or anything, right?" he said. "Just because you helped…"

"Don't worry…I have a new mission now," I said, as I pulled out a notepad with a worn cover, held together with tightly wrapped rubber bands. "I have decided to concentrate on documenting Jo's cases."

"You mean like that famous doctor at Scotland Yard?" he asked.

"Better…'cause I'm a woman," I said, as John stepped out of the room and joined us.

John said that he had to finish a painting job and that Jo wanted to see me. Ken babbled about having to go the office to start on a new case, and Casey decided to seek out some candy. I said my goodbyes to John and Ken, and I yelled a sentence to a running Casey, asking the energetic and renewed boy to come back after he finished his hunting at the vending machines.

I went back inside of the room and confronted an anxious mother who was ready to leave.

"I just told my doctors to get me out of here, and they refused," she said. Her pinched lip said that she was hiding something. I begged for more.

"I got another doctor to check me out, and by the time they figure it out—I will be back at home with my teenager," Jo said, as she pulled back the covers to reveal some pants that she obviously had quickly and recently put on—they were not even wrinkled. It was then that I imagined that Casey might have been involved with getting her clothes to her—or, at least, that was my first assumption. My shock was mixed with a degree of horror when I heard the true explanation.

"I was told that you did a good job," she started. I made the assumption that Ken, or perhaps Casey, had spoken well of me, and I offered a pleasant and surprised smile.

She pulled a black stone out of her pocket and placed it around her neck. I remembered that I once gave it to her for friendship and luck. I picked it up at a local Wiccan tea shop. It was sold as a novelty item to ward off bad things…or so the sticker on it claimed—but an overzealous "believer" told me that it was "magical." Jo kept the stone either in her car or in her pocket, depending upon her mood.

"You tracked me down, despite your first doubts about the paranormal? Guess you can write about all of my adventures now?" she asked me.

I started to object politely, but she said that the doctor told her all about what I had said in the hallway—on his way in to hand her clothes to her. That was when I realized that it was neither Ken or Casey that had spoken well of me.

"What doctor?" I asked. I did not remember seeing any medical staff near us in the hallway.

"The fact that you did not see him means that you are not gifted," she said. "That *rare* time that you *did* see something was caused by—*exceptional* circumstances, I suppose."

"What doctor?" I insisted. I pulled a chair closer and waited for an answer that I suspected but did not want to hear.

"Dr. Pique," Jo said. "He brought in my pants ... and apologized..."

"Wait a minute," I broke in. "Are all of your stories this weird?"

"They seem to be getting worse all of the. . . "—before she could finish, Casey burst into the door and interrupted her.

"Mama!" he exclaimed, out of breath from his sugar trek. "Can we celebrate tonight? I want Ken and Judy to come over also."

"What about John?" she asked and pouted. "Can we invite *him?* I mean, he *is* my boyfriend."

"Oh, really?" he snickered. "You can love *anybody.* I want to celebrate with the people that you actually *like!*"

Jo sighed and ignored his inference, and then she asked for her purse and cell phone in the closet. She called Ken and spoke a few sentences while grabbing a shirt that I tossed to her that was neatly folded on a table beside of her. That was funny, I thought, that wasn't there a moment ago. It was her favorite shirt that she purchased at a yard sale. She considered its price of five cents to be a "steal." It read, "I really don't care!"

"Ken?" she said, with a raised eyebrow and nod, in response to an obvious voicemail message. "Casey and I would like your company tonight...if you can make it."

Jo's eyes twinkled to her son as she closed the phone and said to him, "You like?"

"I like," Casey said, as he grinned. And he added one more word with sincere pronouncement, "Yes!"

We hoped that you enjoyed this short story. Please visit our website at Http://RaeTAlexander.com and feel free to leave a review at Http://www.Amazon.com.

www.ingramcontent.com/pod-product-compliance
Lightning Source LLC
Chambersburg PA
CBHW071212130626

46555CB00004B/1676